D1626843

Jilly always runs ahead.
She can't help herself—she wants to see
what surprises are in store.

Cynthia Cliff

THE WILD GARDEN

PRESTEL

Munich · London · New York

Jilly lives with Grandpa and
Bleu in the village of Mirren.
Here the houses are lined up
in rows upon colorful rows.

Even the village garden has rows upon rows!
Outside the village, things are different.
Here is a tumbling jumble of woods, ponds, and meadows.
This is the wild place. A place full of hidden treasures.
Jilly runs ahead to find them.

In the springtime, Jilly, Grandpa, and Bleu
weave their way between the budding trees.
They search for brand new friends
and delicious edible greens for their supper.

In the village garden, too, spring is a time for new beginnings.
The first flowers of the season bring warm smiles.
There are seedlings to plant and tiny seeds to sow.
The garden *is* carefully planned.

In the wild place, Jilly never knows what she will find.
Sometimes she sees animals, and sometimes they remain out of sight.
But she always knows that they are there.

On a hot summer day, Jilly discovers wild raspberries.
She and Bleu zigzag around like excited bees. They know
that Grandpa will make cool berry ice cream for dessert.

In the heat of summer, the garden is thirsty,
and the work is hard.
The villagers take breaks in the shade
of the orchard.
They know that the sunny days will
mean a good harvest in autumn.

For Jilly, autumn is for jumping in piles of fallen leaves!
But for Grandpa, it is a time for gathering fallen nuts.
All around them, animals prepare for the cold days to come.

In the garden, the villagers also prepare for the cold.
They move delicate plants safely indoors.
They harvest the last fruits and vegetables of the season.
As they work, they start to think about next year's garden.

The days grow cold,
and the wild place becomes quiet and still.
Animals stay cozy in their earthen mazes.
Jilly, Grandpa, and Bleu explore the wintry
meadow. They are grateful for their
warm winter clothes.

After a winter snowstorm, the villagers
gather by the fire to plan their spring garden.
Someone suggests: "What about more
rows and more plants?"
They decide the garden should
be bigger, much bigger!

But Jilly and Grandpa are worried.
What will happen to the nesting spots and the berry patch?
What will happen to the nut trees,
the flower meadows, and the animal dens?
They must do something!

When the snow fades away, a whisper
of green appears in the wild place.
The villagers meet in the garden,
their new plans in hand.
They are going to knock
a hole in the wall.

But what's this! Through the hole,
they see Jilly and Grandpa,
surrounded by a maze of signs
winding around the wild place.

The villagers follow the signs Jilly and Grandpa made.
They meander through the meadow.
They zigzag through the woods. They circle the pond.
In the wild place, they find many surprises.
They see the treasures that make Jilly so
excited to run ahead of Grandpa each day.

In the tall grasses, quiet families graze.

In the meadow, the air is busy
with movement and color.

In the woods, little creatures
have made cozy homes.

Beneath the pond's smooth surface, new life swims about.

And under the budding trees, a happy song calls out to the world.

After that day, the new garden plans are put away.
The villagers decide that a bigger garden might not be a better garden.
Little by little, the wild place creeps in and the village garden tiptoes out.
A new kind of garden emerges, for both people and wildlife—
the wild garden of Mirren.

Jilly and Bleu still run ahead
through the wild place.
But they are not alone.

© 2022, Prestel Verlag, Munich · London · New York
A member of Penguin Random House Verlagsgruppe GmbH
Neumarkter Strasse 28 · 81673 Munich
© text and illustrations: Cynthia Cliff

Library of Congress Control Number: 2021948262
A CIP catalogue record for this book is available from
the British Library.

Editorial direction: Doris Kutschbach
Copy editing: Ayesha Wadhawan, New York
Production management and typesetting: Susanne Hermann
Separations: Reproline Mediateam, Unterföhring
Printing and binding: TBB, a.s., Slovakia
Paper: Magno Natural

ISBN 978-3-7913-7512-0
www.prestel.com

Prestel Publishing compensates the CO$_2$ emissions
produced from the making of this book by supporting
a reforestation project in Brazil. Find further
information on the project here:
www.ClimatePartner.com/14044-1912-1001

FSC
www.fsc.org

MIX
Paper from
responsible sources
FSC® C022120

Our production is
climate neutral
ClimatePartner.com/14044-1912-1001
Print product

Penguin Random House Verlagsgruppe FSC® N001967